The HighBreed and Vilgax are no longer a threat, and the Omnitrix has been destroyed.

Ben Tennyson is now 16 years old, and he must learn the secrets of the new Ultimatrix to battle alien attacks led by the evil Aggregor.

Ben can tap into all of his original powers with the Ultimatrix, but he can also upgrade his alien forms into even **STRONGER** and more **POWERFUL** versions – 'ultimate' aliens.

Join the action as Ben goes hero again – ultimate style!

NOW READ ON ...

MEET THE CHARACTERS

Ben Tennyson
He's always
ready for action

Gwen Tennyson
Ben's cousin,
with magical
powers

Kevin E. Levin
He is tough and
strong

Max Tennyson
Ben and Gwen's
Grandpa

Sandra Tennyson
Ben's mum

Swampfire
He can shoot
scorching flames

Big Chill
This cool guy
breathes ice

Ultimate Big Chill
He can create
ice flames

Humungousaur
He's a massive
dino-alien

Nanomech
He's like a tiny machine

Jet Ray
He has poisonous stingers on his head

Spidermonkey
He can stick to walls

Cannonbolt
He is covered in tough armour plating

Lodestar
His power is magnetic

Vulkanus
A bad guy in a huge robotic suit

Charmcaster
She's a villain with magic powers

Zombozo
He's a nasty, scary clown

Will Harangue
This newsreader doesn't like Ben

Oliver
He works for Will Harangue

EGMONT

We bring stories to life

First published in Great Britain 2011
by Egmont UK Limited
239 Kensington High Street
London W8 6SA

CARTOON NETWORK, the logo, BEN 10 ULTIMATE ALIEN
and all related characters and elements are trademarks
of and © 2011 Cartoon Network.

Adapted by Matt Yeo

ISBN 978 1 4052 5705 3

1 3 5 7 9 10 8 6 4 2

Printed and bound in Great Britain

The Forest Stewardship Council (FSC) is an international,
non-governmental organisation dedicated to promoting responsible
management of the world's forests. FSC operates a system of forest
certification and product labelling that allows consumers to identify
wood and wood-based products from well-managed forests.

For more information about Egmont's paper buying policy,
please visit www.egmont.co.uk/ethicalpublishing
For more information about the FSC, please visit
their website at www.fsc.org

WHERE THEY LIVE

CHAPTER ONE

SNEAK ATTACK

It was a quiet evening in the street. The only sound coming from the Tennysons' kitchen was of pots and pans being washed. Ben's mum, Sandra, had her headphones on and was humming along to her favourite songs, unaware of the danger she was in.

Some red laser dots drifted across her brow, settling in the centre of her forehead. From a corner of the Tennysons' back garden, the famous bounty hunter SevenSeven powered up his weapons. One strong blast would soon get rid of the target.

A voice from behind the villain was enough to him off.

'Hey, SevenSeven!' growled Grandpa Max, his own high-tech weapons pointing at the intruder. 'You want to pick a fight with somebody, try me!'

SevenSeven turned around and fired a storm of energy blasts. Max ducked, shooting back and taking cover.

In the kitchen, Sandra's music drowned out the battle outside.

SevenSeven threw plasma

discs at Max, knocking away his weapons. Max dived behind a tree.

'My daughter-in-law is not a target!' he yelled to SevenSeven.

But Max had taken his eyes off the villain for a second too long. SevenSeven blasted the tree with razor-sharp metal darts. Max lunged for his enemy, but was knocked to the ground.

'**Uggh!**' he groaned, landing with a thud.

As Max looked up, SevenSeven withdrew his blasters, his hands turning into deadly buzz saws.

SevenSeven ran straight at Max, swinging his blades. Max moved fast and grabbed one of the metal darts stuck in the tree. Throwing the dart as hard as he could, Max hit the alien in his power pack, sending sparks into the air.

Suddenly, SevenSeven's armour began to glow and shudder. A low whine came from his suit and then a **BANG!** as his jetpack burst. The alien disappeared into the night sky in a cloud of smoke.

Max looked back at Sandra at the window. She was still unaware of what had happened.

'I've got to find some way to stop this insanity,' Max muttered, 'before it's too late ...'

As the train thundered down the track, a battle on a carriage roof was about to derail the entire train.

From out of nowhere, Rath flew through the air, landing with a loud thud. Picking himself up from the dented roof of the carriage, he bared his teeth at his attackers.

'Let me tell you something, Rojo,' he snarled, pointing a clawed fist at the sky. 'Nobody robs a train when Rath is on the job!'

Hovering overhead, the villain Rojo and two biker gang members circled Ben's alien. They each rode a flying motorcycle and carried a glowing energy chain.

One of the bikers sped towards Rath, hooking the alien's arm with her chain. Rath was dragged, face down, towards the last carriage. With just seconds to spare before Rath was toast, the chain that held him was broken. Glinting in the sunlight, Kevin stood on top of the train. He had turned himself into living metal, with a sharpened axe for a hand.

Rath continued to bounce along the carriages, towards the edge of the train. Fortunately, Gwen had conjured up a glowing energy platform in the nick of time, saving her cousin's life.

Just then, there was another roar of engines from above.

'Heads up!' yelled Kevin as two of the bikers screamed into view, dragging an energy chain between their vehicles.

Digging his clawed feet into

the carriage roof, Rath surprised his attackers by grabbing the chain, causing their bikes to smash into each other. As the screeching sound of metal filled the air, a powerful explosion sent the bikers tumbling from the sky. Kevin and Gwen snatched the bikers' weapons.

Rojo revved up her bike, ready to escape. Rath tossed a piece of metal from one of the smashed motorcycles towards her. The metal struck and sliced through Rojo's engine. The bike exploded in a shower of metal and fuel, sending the villain crashing down onto the top of the train.

'Nice shot!' grinned Gwen.

Minutes later, the train shuddered to a stop at the city railway station. Rojo and her gang were safely captured and quickly led to jail.

In a blinding flash of green light, Rath changed back into 16-year-old Ben Tennyson.

'All's well that ends well!' he smiled. 'Anyway, this is our stop.'

A crowd of news reporters, cameras and fans were awaiting the three heroes. Ever since his true identity had been revealed to the world, Ben received constant attention.

'It's him!' came a cry from the

crowd. 'What happened?' asked a reporter, thrusting a microphone into Ben's face.

'My adoring public awaits,' smiled Ben.

But they were interrupted by a blast of air and the low rumble of an approaching aircraft. Max's familiar green plane – the Rustbucket III – lowered carefully onto the train tracks, sending dust spinning around the waiting crowd.

'Aw, not now,' moaned Ben. Just when he was having his five

minutes of fame …

The plane's access hatch opened to reveal a serious-looking Max. He waved to the others to get on board. 'Now!' he scowled.

CHAPTER TWO

NO LAUGHING MATTER

Minutes later the high-tech craft was in the air.

'What was so important it couldn't wait until after my interview?' Ben moaned.

Max wasn't impressed. 'Your newfound fame is the problem,' he growled, still nursing his wound from the battle with SevenSeven.

'How?' asked Gwen.

'Ever since the world found out about your powers,' Max explained, 'a lot of your old enemies have been trying to get revenge by hurting those close to you.'

Confused, Ben shrugged off his Grandpa's comments. 'Like who? I haven't seen anyone.'

'And I was hoping to keep it that way,' Max replied. 'So far I've been able to deal with them without your folks knowing about it.'

Max paused for a second. He seemed exhausted. '... but now ... I can't do this alone any more.'

Gwen hated seeing her Grandpa like this. 'You should never have been alone, Grandpa. You should've let us help.'

Ben agreed. 'All you had to do was tell us.'

'You kids have enough to worry about,' said Max.

Gwen was concerned. 'This isn't right. There are supposed to be rules. Family is off-limits.'

'At first I thought the attacks were random,' said Max, 'but I was wrong. They're organised.'

Ben was curious. 'Organised? By who ...?'

Miles away at an abandoned circus, fairground rides lay rusting and torn flags fluttered lazily in the night air. This creepy place had been deserted for years.

Lurking inside the darkness of the main circus tent were two figures, their faces lit by a single candle.

'He said he was going to be here,' a voice mumbled. In the dim light, the alien known as Vulkanus stepped towards the smaller figure.

'Well, he's not,' snapped Charmcaster, 'and I don't wait around for anybody.'

Charmcaster the witch stopped. The hairs on the back of her neck stood up. She could feel that something, or someone, was standing right behind her.

'Zombozo ...?' said Charmcaster, her voice shaking.

'My apologies,' murmured the freaky clown. 'I'm usually on time, but I got caught up in my work.'

Zombozo was carrying a

shovel, covered in fresh soil.

'Good help is so hard to find,' said Zombozo eerily. 'Particularly if you carefully bury the remains.'

Tossing the shovel to one side, he stepped closer to the flickering candle.

'Yeah, yeah, we get it,' Vulkanus said. You're creepy and dangerous,' he muttered. 'That hasn't got your people any closer to Tennyson's family.'

Zombozo moved silently to stand before the alien.

'True. And that's why I've asked you here,' replied Zombozo, patting Vulkanus' surprised face. 'I'm taking matters into my own hands, and I need you two to help.'

'So what do we do?' Vulkanus asked. 'Every time anybody attacks

Tennyson's home, they're beaten.'

'Then the answer is simple,' said Charmcaster. 'We don't attack them at home. We wait until they're not expecting us.'

'That's it, Charmcaster,' said Zombozo. 'Now we're thinkin' like a team. ***Bwa-ha, ha, ha!***'

The clown's creepy chuckle echoed around the tent.

The next morning was bright and sunny. In the Tennysons' living room, Ben's mum was doing her exercises, using a large rubber ball. Ben sat nearby.

'Err … everything OK?' Ben asked, as his mother leaned backwards on the ball.

'My body and spirit are in total

balance, son,' she replied, just as she overbalanced and thudded to the floor. *Whoops!*

Ben dashed over to help his mum up.

'Well, my spirit is in total balance, at least,' Sandra grinned, rubbing her leg. 'Why do you keep asking me if I'm OK? Is everything all right with you?'

Ben paused. 'Me? Sure. It's just … I, ah, hear there's this nasty flu going around and …'

Sandra was about to reply

when they both heard the rumble of an engine in the driveway. Ben moved to the front door, in time to see his father's car pulling away from the house.

'Hey, where's Dad going?' he asked, quickly.

'He's picking up a new grow lamp,' replied Sandra. 'Why?'

'Does he really need to go?' said Ben.

'We don't want the plants to die,' Sandra replied. She had no idea how worried Ben was, following the recent attacks. He needed to keep a closer eye on his parents, and make sure they were safe at all times.

Ben grabbed his mobile phone and dialled. There was no way he was going to let anything happen to his family.

CHAPTER THREE

The Twisted Trap

Ben's dad, Carl, drove along a quiet country road. As he came towards a tight bend, he didn't see the sharp, shiny objects scattered on the road.

The metal spikes tore through his car's tyres, shredding them in an instant. Carl struggled with the steering wheel, slammed on the brakes and skidded to a stop.

Carl climbed out of the car and stared at his torn tyres. 'What next?' he muttered, head in hands.

Vulkanus, Charmcaster and Zombozo were looking on nearby, hidden by the thick forest trees. This was no accident. They had placed the spikes on the road.

Zombozo grinned to himself. Perfect, just perfect.

The three villains watched as Carl changed the tyres on his car with spares from his boot.

'See, what'd I tell ya?' boasted Zombozo. 'It was easy to stop him. Now who wants the first go at him?'

But the evil clown's plan was about to hit a dead end.

'Only way to get to him, ugly,' said a voice from behind, 'is by going through us.'

Turning quickly, the three villains stared into the faces of their enemies – Ben, Gwen and Kevin!

Zombozo reached into his jacket and pulled out a spray can. One touch of the button on its lid, and a jet of bright green liquid blasted through the air towards Ben and the others. As it hit the grass and trees, the liquid sizzled, eating through everything it touched.

'That's acid!' shouted Kevin as Gwen managed to create an energy shield in the nick of time.

Zombozo's can sputtered and stopped spraying. It was broken. Charmcaster stepped forward.

'I've waited a long time for a rematch, Gwen,' she said, and tossed a handful of seeds onto the grass in front of her. Charmcaster yelled some magic words, and the seeds sprouted, planted roots, and grew to a monstrous size. Within seconds, thick green roots had sprouted from underground, wrapping themselves around Gwen, Ben and Kevin.

'*Ugh!*' exclaimed Gwen as the vines squeezed the breath from her.

Now it was Vulkanus' turn. 'You're out of your depth,' he yelled, raising a blaster pistol at Ben.

But before he could pull the

trigger, Ben wriggled free from the roots. He slapped the Ultimatrix on his wrist.

'Tell it to … Swampfire!' he shouted as a blinding green flash turned him into the plant-like alien.

Vulkanus shot out a bolt of blue energy, but Swampfire quickly fought back with a powerful flame blast. The two beams collided in mid-air, before Swampfire's flame hit Vulkanus with full force.

'*ARGH!*' Vulkanus crashed into the surrounding trees.

Swampfire then went after Zombozo. Having fixed his spray can, the clown aimed another blast of acid at his enemy.

Meanwhile, Kevin had absorbed the solid strength of rock. He turned his hand into a sharp blade and cut through Gwen's leafy chains. Having freed Gwen, Kevin leapt towards Charmcaster, knocking her to the ground with a single blow.

Before she could move or cast a spell to save herself, the witch was trapped in a glowing energy cage. Looking up, she glared at Gwen who was using her powers to trap the villain.

Swampfire and Zombozo carried on fighting. The clown fired a shot that hit Swampfire's arm, melting it off. That wasn't a problem for Swampfire though, as he simply grew it right back!

Next, a fiery bolt knocked the spray can out of the clown's grasp. Kevin stepped up to Zombozo, turning his hand into a huge stone mallet. He smashed the mallet into the ground with terrific force, sending the clown flying.

Vulkanus tried to stand up, but was knocked to the ground again by a blast from Swampfire.

'**Ahhh!**' he grunted in pain.

'**Ugh!**' moaned Charmcaster as she took a pounding from Gwen.

Zombozo could tell that they were being beaten. He got to his feet and dusted himself down.

'That's it, gang, we're leaving!' he barked to his partners.

Vulkanus and Charmcaster staggered to their feet, rubbing their bruises.

Zombozo then released a small red balloon into the air. It began to grow and within seconds it was huge. Suddenly, with a loud *'POP!'* the balloon exploded, showering the forest with colourful confetti. By the time the confetti had settled, the villains had disappeared.

Covered in the colourful streamers, Ben changed back to his human form and looked around for signs of the bad guys.

'Got to give him credit,' said Gwen. 'He really improved his bag of tricks.'

Ben looked confused. 'We've fought him before?'

'Yes! You used to be afraid of clowns,' said Gwen. She smiled as she remembered Ben's childhood fear. 'Don't you remember?'

But Ben had no memory of it. 'Huh. Doesn't ring a bell. We fight a lot of people,' he shrugged.

'Scared of clowns,' Kevin chuckled. 'Priceless!'

Ben dashed to the edge of the forest to check on his father.

'Right now, I'm scared that Dad ...' he began. But Carl had replaced his tyres and was driving away, totally unaware of what had just happened.

'He never knew he was in danger,' said Gwen.

'And I'm going to make sure we keep it that way,' muttered Ben through gritted teeth.

Later, back at the fairground, the three villains were feeling sorry for themselves. Vulkanus had shed his armour and was making some repairs to it, his tiny 'real' body scurrying around the bulky high-tech suit.

'So much for teamwork,' he growled, polishing a burn mark on the armour.

Charmcaster was angry that they'd backed away from the fight.

'I could have beaten Gwen,'

she yelled, 'if you'd just let me.'

But the clown wasn't worried.

'No, no, no,' he shook his head. 'You're looking at this the wrong way. We learnt a great deal from that battle,' said Zombozo. 'I finally know exactly how to put an end to Tennyson and company.'

'We're listening, clown,' said Charmcaster.

Zombozo licked his lips.

'Have either of you ever heard the term "divide and conquer"? *Bwa-ha, ha, ha!*'

The next day, Gwen and her Aunt Sandra were doing the grocery shopping. Sandra usually did this on her own, but Ben had told Gwen to go with her this time, for safety.

'We don't spend nearly enough time together, Aunt Sandra,' Gwen said. 'I wouldn't have missed this for the world.'

Sandra was happy to be out with her niece. They hadn't had a girls' day out in ages. She smiled as they returned to the car and started to put the shopping away.

Suddenly, there was a shrieking sound. Charmcaster had arrived at the car park, together with six huge rock monsters. With a flick of her wrist, Charmcaster gave her orders and the monsters stomped towards Gwen.

'Stay behind me, Aunt Sandra,' Gwen warned. 'I'll keep you safe!'

The first few rock monsters were knocked down by a storm of mystical blasts thrown by Gwen.

Charmcaster was angry with her rock army. 'She's just one girl!' she yelled.

Another wave of rock monsters ran at Gwen, and were turned into piles of smoking rubble. With the army beaten, Gwen faced her real foe.

But the witch conjured a rod from thin air and aimed deadly blasts at Gwen.

Holding up an energy shield, Gwen avoided the attack. 'Your old power-draining trick won't work this time,' she began, 'I'm way better at magic that I used to b–'

A clammy hand on her shoulder suddenly stopped Gwen.

'Huh?' she whispered, knowing exactly who the hand belonged to.

Zombozo had quietly crept up behind Gwen.

'You really oughta watch where you're goin', missy,' the clown muttered.

Electricity shot through Gwen's body as Zombozo used his

trick buzzer to knock her out.

'Yagh!' she screamed.

It was all Gwen could do to keep her eyes open and watch helplessly as Zombozo grabbed Aunt Sandra. Charmcaster landed in front of Gwen, and began to lift up her wooden rod to cast a final spell on Gwen.

But Zombozo made her stop. 'C'mon, we got what we came for,' said the clown.

From behind Charmcaster, Vulkanus appeared from nowhere,

and snatched the mystical rod from her hands.

'Got her, boss,' he growled, lifting Charmcaster off the ground with his free hand.

Zombozo dragged Ben's mother kicking and screaming out of the car park.

'Gwen! Help!' Sandra yelled.

Gwen staggered weakly to her feet and tried to chase the villains. 'Ugh … Aunt Sandra …' she groaned, but it was no use. The blast had taken away all her energy, and the last thing she saw was the terrible trio escaping with their precious prize …

CHAPTER FOUR

Fatal Attractions

Hours later, at the Tennyson house, Gwen still had a throbbing headache from her battle. And Ben wasn't helping by yelling at her.

'You lost her? You lost her?' he shouted again and again, 'You were supposed to protect her!'

Gwen held her head in her hands and began to apologise.

'I tried, Ben, really. I … I'm sorry,' she replied.

'"Sorry" doesn't get my mother back,' Ben snapped.

Kevin stepped between the two cousins.

'Give Gwen a break,' he said. 'She feels bad enough.'

'It's not your mother they kidnapped,' Ben yelled.

Kevin wasn't going to let Ben feel sorry for himself.

'If it were me, I wouldn't stand here blaming people,' he said. 'I'd go and get her back!'

Ben realised he'd gone too far. He wasn't really angry with Gwen. He was angry about what had happened and he felt helpless. And he was worried about his mother.

'I'm sorry, Gwen,' Ben apologised to his cousin.

She patted his arm gently. 'We'll find her.'

Kevin wasn't so sure. 'How? With a tracking device? With one of Gwen's spells?' he asked.

'Zombozo took her,' Ben thought out loud. 'I know exactly where to look.'

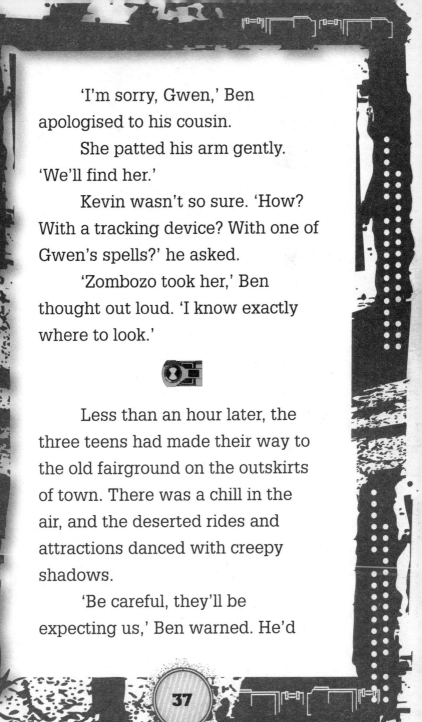

Less than an hour later, the three teens had made their way to the old fairground on the outskirts of town. There was a chill in the air, and the deserted rides and attractions danced with creepy shadows.

'Be careful, they'll be expecting us,' Ben warned. He'd

remembered the old fairground and he had a really strong feeling that Zombozo would be there.

Ben, Gwen and Kevin went their separate ways, each of them taking a different route into the theme park. Suddenly a loud scream pierced the night air. It was Sandra!

Ben ran towards his mother's voice, pushing through a rickety wooden door leading into the Hall of Mirrors. He was greeted by twisted images of himself in the tall, dirty mirrors. The place hadn't been used for years, and the smell of stale candyfloss filled the room.

'Mum?' Ben shouted, but there was no one around.

Heading for the exit, Ben did not notice the shadowy figures coming out of the darkness …

In another part of the creepy fairground, Kevin slipped past the motionless horses of the merry-go-round.

'I used to love fairground rides,' he muttered to himself. 'Now they just make me sick.'

'You have the same effect on me!' came a familiar voice from above him.

Kevin looked up. Charmcaster was standing at the very top of the towering old rollercoaster.

'Where's Ben's mum?' he shouted up to her.

'Where's Gwen?' Charmcaster shouted back.

Kevin grabbed a nearby steel pillar and took on its qualities.

'Probably kicking butt,' he yelled. 'Kinda like what I'm gonna do to you!'

Charmcaster was ready for him and held up her mystical rod that glowed with energy.

'Talk is cheap,' she sneered, ready to beat Kevin once and for all.

Gwen's route led her to the main circus tent. As Gwen walked inside, a dazzling spotlight snapped on. Zombozo stood with his back to her, arms outstretched as he greeted an invisible audience.

'Ladies and gentlemen and victims of all ages,' he boomed at the empty seats. 'Welcome to the final act. I promise it'll be a … KILLER!'

He turned around sharply and glared at Gwen. Whatever his evil plan was, she was about to find out.

'*Bwa-ha, ha, ha!*' he chuckled through yellow teeth.

CHAPTER FIVE

Final Curtain Call

Back in the Hall of Mirrors, Ben noticed another reflection and moved quickly. He was just in time to avoid Vulkanus' attack.

'Shouldn't try to sneak up on someone in a Hall of Mirrors,' Ben said, activating the Ultimatrix.

The blinding green flash cleared, revealing Ben's chosen alien form – Big Chill! Frosted air filled the room as he fixed his attacker with a glare.

'Where is my mother, Vulkanus?' he demanded.

'Where you'll never find her,' the villain replied.

He clapped his hands together. The shockwave shattered the nearby mirrors, revealing an army of mining trolls. Each of the creatures carried a razor-sharp axe and they headed straight for Big Chill.

At the rollercoaster, Kevin and Charmcaster's battle had begun with the witch blasting the ground around his feet into craters.

'You're not a very good shot,' he scoffed.

But Charmcaster wasn't aiming at Kevin.

'Don't have to be,' she replied. 'I cheat.'

As she spoke, rock monsters began to emerge from the craters, dragging their stony bodies up to face Kevin. Now he was in trouble!

Gwen was taking no chances with Zombozo and had surrounded herself with a protective shield.

'Where's Ben's mum?' she demanded from behind the shield.

'Like I'd just tell you,' the clown chuckled.

'You never were much of a threat, clown,' Gwen replied, lowering her shield and preparing to send a powerful energy blast in his direction.

Zombozo just grinned and raised his arm at her. 'That was then, girlie. This is now.'

With a puff of smoke and a loud **SPRONG!** the clown's arm stretched the length of the circus tent, his fist coming within inches of Gwen's face. The clown then reached for another weapon. It looked like a harmless party popper, but Gwen knew better than that.

Green bands shot from the party popper and wrapped around her arms. She was tied up tight and couldn't move. Gwen was Zombozo's prisoner!

Outside, Kevin was battling the rock monsters when one of

them crashed into him. They both stumbled and fell against the controls of a fairground ride. It came to life, spinning and whirling as the two enemies fought. Kevin hit out at the monster.

'Get – **ugh** – off me!' he grunted, thumping the rock monsters back into the ground from where they'd come.

Watching from the top of the rollercoaster, Charmcaster pointed her rod directly at Kevin's head. He ducked and escaped the blast. 'Missed again!' Kevin yelled, stopping in front of a windmill ride.

Charmcaster shot out a more powerful blast. The energy struck the windmill itself and its creaking sails suddenly spun into life. The windmill ripped away from its base and thundered towards the rollercoaster, smashing rock monsters in its path. The windmill then crashed into the ride Charmcaster was standing on.

With a groan of twisting metal and splintering wood, the old rollercoaster collapsed, crashing to the ground in a cloud of dust. Watching from a safe distance, Kevin turned back to his human form, satisfied with his work.

Meanwhile, back in the circus tent, Gwen was struggling to escape from her trap.

'**Ugh!**' she moaned, as the green bands seemed to get tighter.

Zombozo shuffled over to her, clearly pleased with his handiwork.

'Oh, Gwenny-Gwenny-Gwenny,' he whispered, 'you're wasting your strength. My magic streamers are like steel!'

She was helpless and Zombozo knew it.

'So many ways to get rid of you,' the clown muttered to himself. 'What to do? What to do ...?'

In the Hall of Mirrors, Big Chill sent out blast after frozen blast, trapping the trolls in blocks of ice. But as soon as he froze one group, more began to spill out of the mirrors like an army of deadly ants.

'It's time to go … **ULTIMATE!**' Big Chill shouted.

Tapping the symbol on his chest, Big Chill changed into something even more powerful. 'Ultimate Big Chill!' he yelled.

Vulkanus looked worried. He'd never met this alien before.

'You're tough with an army behind you, Vulkanus,' Ultimate Big Chill rasped. 'But now it's just you, me, and fire so cold, it **BURNS!**'

An icy blast came from his mouth as Ultimate Big Chill froze the entire troll army in its tracks. Vulkanus was also half trapped in the ice. He wasn't going anywhere.

Ultimate Big Chill floated towards him, preparing to let out another frosty blast.

Vulkanus raised his hand. He was ready to give up. 'If you want the lady back, I'll tell you where she is. Please don't hurt –'

'For once, stop talking,' Ultimate Big Chill said, before trapping Vulkanus up to his neck in freezing ice.

'OK …' sighed the tired and defeated villain.

Just then, Kevin wandered into the smashed Hall of Mirrors.

'Nice work, Ben,' he nodded at Vulkanus. 'I've taken care of Charmcaster.'

As the words left Kevin's mouth they both realised there was someone missing.

'That means Gwen's with …' Ben began, but Kevin knew all too well.

'C'mon!' Kevin yelled. If anything happened to Gwen, he'd never forgive himself.

The big top echoed with Zombozo's creepy laughter as he stood over Gwen. The clown leaned in closer. Gwen could smell his revolting breath on her face.

'This isn't just about beating your cousin,' Zombozo said. 'It's about making him suffer.'

Zombozo pointed at the roof of the big top. Gwen gazed up at a single figure, high on the tightrope wire. She knew who it was, and it filled her with fear.

'Aunt Sandra!' she yelled at the person they'd come to rescue.

'Gwen? Is that you?' replied Sandra. She had both feet on the high wire and was just about able to stay steady with the help of a long pole. 'Please help! I don't know how long I can keep my balance ...'

'You've got about two minutes,' Zombozo grinned.

At that moment there was a loud **BANG!** as a small explosion went off above them. Zombozo had planted a small bomb up there and it had set fire to the rope that held

Sandra up. The flames began to lick along the wire, getting closer to Sandra who wobbled back and forth on the tightrope.

Gwen had had enough. Her eyes glowed with energy and she gritted her teeth as she used her powers to set herself free.

Zombozo turned around. 'Huh? How'd you ...?' he began to ask, as Gwen came towards him, her eyes shining with energy.

'You have no idea who you're dealing with,' she said, moving even closer to Zombozo. 'I want you to listen to me, then pass on the message to every lowlife you know.'

The clown felt uneasy as he realised he was being threatened by Gwen.

'If you want to come after Ben, or Kevin, or me, fine,' she continued. 'That's the life we chose.'

Zombozo couldn't even see the outline of Gwen's human form as she shone like a pink star, her energy powers having changed her entire body. Zombozo had to shield his eyes from the light.

'I'm talking to you. Look at me!' she demanded, with a strange sound to her voice.

Zombozo peeled his fingers from his face and peeked at her.

'As of right now,' she warned

him, 'if any of you ever attacks one of our family, or even bumps into someone we love in the street ...'

As she talked, Gwen grew in size and strength until she towered over the pathetic clown.

'... this is what awaits you!' Gwen finished and the clown's eyes filled with pure terror.

'RRRRGH!' Zombozo screamed.

With Sandra safe, Gwen sat down with her aunt to munch on some fresh candyfloss she'd managed to find.

'You sure you don't want any?' she asked her aunt.

'Thank you, but processed sugar is poison,' said Sandra, thinking of her exercise routine.

Ben and Kevin rushed into the circus tent.

'Hey, guys,' Gwen waved at the boys. Ben's eyes lit up.

'Gwen! Mum! Are you all right?' he yelled, bounding over.

'I'm fine, dear,' Sandra said. 'I'm just a little concerned about Gwen's diet though.'

Kevin looked around the tent. 'Where's Zombozo?' he asked.

'You don't have to worry about him any more,' said Gwen. 'We, erm … made a deal.'

Ben and Kevin looked at each other with their eyebrows raised.

Who knew what had really happened in that circus tent that night …?